The Faith Of Little Nell

DOROTHY STRANGE

DEDICATION

To those who believe in others as they believe in that one special person.

CONTENTS

Acknowledgments

1 PARADISE COURT

2 A FOGGY NIGHT

3 HER FIRST PRAYER

4 A PRISONER

5 MEMORIES OF THE PAST

6 FORGIVING AND FORGIVEN

7 NELLIE'S SECRET

8 THE POT OF SNOWDROPS

9 LOST

10 THE MESSAGE OF THE LILIES

11 PHYLLIS FINDS A HOME

12 ON THE YORKSHIRE COAST

13 CAN IT BE?

14 FOUND!

15 SAFE HOME FOR NELL'S SAKE

ACKNOWLEDGMENTS

To my friends, my family, but above all to those strangers who have crossed my path and whom I will one day meet.

CHAPTER 1

PARADISE COURT

A strange paradise indeed was the narrow, dirty, dingy court in Bloomsbury, known by this name.

Very little sunshine ever found its way between the tall houses, though from time to time a few stray beams did penetrate the gloom, and shed some brightness around; but this only happened occasionally; as a rule the place looked dismal to the last degree. To add to the general discomfort, clothes were often to be seen hanging on lines across the court, though it was a mystery how any linen ever got clean in that smoky atmosphere.

In this dreary, sunless spot little Nell was born and brought up.

Her childhood had had no brightness in it. She had never known what it was to run about in country lanes; she had never picked the wild flowers, nor played in the green fields like other children.

Her father was a costermonger, who sold fruit and vegetables when he had money to buy them. Too often he spent, in the public-house at night, all the money he earned in the day, leaving his wife and child to fare as best they could.

Mrs. Jackson went out charring or washing, and so managed to pick up a scanty living; but it was a hard life, and she would sometimes think with regret of the happy days before her marriage, and of the old home in the Yorkshire village. She had grown spiritless and weary, and she was often cross with her little girl, who had been delicate from her birth, and who was never likely to earn her own living.

Nellie was a pale, sickly child, with a somewhat pinched and careworn look on her small face; but she had big, brown, earnest eyes, in which there was a wistful, pathetic look, such as one sometimes sees in a dog; a sort of pleading for love and kindness.

She had also a quantity of dark, curly hair growing all over her head; this and her fine eyes redeemed her face from being plain and uninteresting.

Small for her age, she might easily have passed for eight, though in reality she was ten years old.

She had sometimes attended a ragged school in the neighbourhood, but her weak health often prevented her walking so far, thus she had only mastered a few words and could read but little. To a Sunday school she had never gone, and the only good influence of her life, up to the present time, was her love for one of the neighbours in the court, one who was poor indeed in this world's goods, but "rich in faith." This poor seamstress, who spent all her days, and most of her nights, making shirts, pitied the poor child, and would often let her sit beside her while she worked. Sometimes Nell would run an errand for her friend, and then Betsy Martin would give her a slice of bread, all the payment she could afford. While the child sat by her, Betsy would tell her a Bible story, or teach her some text which had brought comfort to her own heart. These were golden hours in the life of the lonely child, who often found her way into her kind neighbour's room.

When Nell was nine years old, a baby sister had been given her, and for six months this little one had proved a true sunbeam to the lonely child. From the first Nell had had the entire charge of "Baby Jess," Mrs. Jackson being out at work all day. But, alas! "Baby Jess" did not thrive in the dingy atmosphere of Paradise Court. Perhaps little Nell hardly understood the management of so young a baby, and occasionally under—or overfed it. Certain it was that "Nell's baby," as the neighbours called it, soon began to droop, gradually fading away, till one evening, six months after it had entered the court, the little spirit took its flight to a brighter, purer land, "above the bright blue sky."

For many weeks Nellie refused to be comforted for the loss of her baby sister, and more and more lonely grew her life. She was not strong enough to join in the rough games of the other children in the court, so day by day she would sit on the doorstep of the dwelling, in which was the one room she called home, wishing she had something to do, and longing to be strong and hearty like the children around her.

She was sitting thus one chilly afternoon in November, feeling very sad and lonely, for her father had been drinking more than usual of late, when Jim Turner, the bully of the neighbourhood, and her special terror, came up and accosted her.

"Well, pale face, how goes the world with you? Yer looks hungry; have a bite of this 'ere bun!"

Nellie was not accustomed to such generosity from Jim, and at once the truth flashed across her mind, the bun had been stolen. Hungry she truly was, yet though sadly ignorant, she knew that stealing was wrong, so summoning all her courage, she said,

"I be hungry, there's no mistake; but, Jim yer stole that bun, and I won't touch it."

Indignant at being found out, Jim made a

dart at the child, saying,

"Yer'll eat it, or I'll do for you."

But before he could reach her, Nell had slipped past him, up the staircase of the next house. If she could only get to Betsy, who was just now ill in bed, she would be safe from her tormentor.

Breathless and panting, she reached the top landing, and was just going to push open the door, when she was arrested by some strange sounds. Somebody was singing in Betsy's room. Who could it be? She knew Betsy could not sing; she could only hum a few tunes.

How lovely it was! Nellie had never heard singing like that before. The door was ajar, and the child went nearer.

She stood entranced, forgetting her recent fright, for there, sitting by the bedside, was a young, and what to her seemed a beautiful lady. She was singing to Betsy, whose closed eyes and calm face showed her keen enjoyment.

Who could it be? Nell had never seen a lady in the court before. What could it mean?

What it meant and who it was must be left to another chapter to explain.

CHAPTER 2

A FOGGY NIGHT

In a small street, turning out of Russell Square, lived a mother and her two children, a son and a daughter.

Left a widow very early in life, with small means, it had been Mrs. Moore's chief endeavour to train her children well, and to give them a good education.

Evelyn, now nineteen, had well repaid her mother's tender care, and was her constant companion, her right hand in everything; while Harold, a lad of seventeen, still at school, gave promise of being the comfort of her old age. For some years Mrs. Moore had been an invalid, and thus on Evelyn had devolved most of the household cares and duties.

Let us today enter the little sitting-room, in which a bright fire is burning, making it look cheerful in spite of the thick fog outside.

The mother and daughter are alone; Evelyn in her favourite place, on a footstool at her mother's feet, is saying,

"You will let me visit a few sick people, if Mrs. Green chooses them for me, won't you, mother dear? I am sure I could manage this even with my daily teaching, and it would be such a pleasure."

"I am quite willing you should undertake this, my child, if it can be done without neglecting any home duty, or overdoing your strength; but Harold must never feel you are too busy or too tired to make his evenings bright, for remember home work comes before any other."

"You shall never have cause to complain of this, mother, if you consent. The sight of the sorrow around me will only make me love my dear home more than ever. Trust me, mother."

"Well, darling, try it! Begin with the one case Mrs. Green told us of today, that poor seamstress in Paradise Court; hers seems a sad case, and they evidently have no district visitor there; but remember, dear, I cannot have you undertaking to visit the whole court: you are too young for this at present."

"I will do nothing without your leave, mother; will that satisfy you? So tomorrow I may go and see Betsy Martin, and may I take her some of that soup we had for dinner?"

"If there is any left, but I want some for Harold tonight; if there is none, you shall take her a little pudding. Now ring for tea, and we will have the gas lighted. Harold ought to be home by this time, and he will like to find tea ready."

The shutters were closed, the gas was lighted, the tea was brought in, but no Harold came. After waiting for more than an hour, Evelyn insisted on giving her mother her tea, saying she must wait no longer. It was a silent meal, for both women were anxious about the boy who was out so late that foggy evening.

At last, about seven o'clock, the hall door opened quickly, and the next moment Harold entered, saying,

"I hope you haven't been frightened, mother, I was detained. I could not help it, as you shall hear directly." And he leaned over his mother's couch and kissed her.

"We feared you had lost your way, my son, and are thankful to see you safe home."

"Oh no, mother! No fear of my losing my way; I know every step, even in a fog. If Eve will give me my tea, I will tell you all about it.

"I was coming home by a short cut, through a narrow street, when I saw a man lying on the pavement, apparently very ill. I stopped to see what I could do to help him. I soon saw that it was a case of drink; but as the fellow was helpless, I couldn't leave him like that, so I called a man who was passing, and I asked him to lend me a hand to get him to a place of safety. I was wondering where I could take him, not wishing to land him in the Lock-up for the night, when someone standing by said, 'That's Tom Jackson of Paradise Court.' I asked where that might be, and finding it was near, we half led, half dragged the man to his court, which was truly a Paradise lost!'

"You never saw such a place; it seemed full of squalling children, noisy women, and quarrel-some men.

"We found No. 4, and gave him into the care of a man who said he lived in the same house. But all this took time, and I was afraid you would be getting anxious. Oh, mother! How thankful I was you had brought me up an abstainer. I should be sorry to touch the stuff that made Jackson what I saw him today.

"A poor, half-starved girl came down the stairs; they said she was Jackson's child. How I pitied her! Now, Eve, another cup of tea, please, and then I'll get to work and make up for lost time."

Evelyn did not dare to look at her mother during this description of Paradise Court. It must be confessed it was not an inviting prospect.

"You were quite right, Harold, to do what you could for the man. Such things are sad indeed in a Christian land. We must try and get hold of the poor fellow when he is sober."

Then turning to Evelyn, Mrs. Moore said,

"I don't much like your going alone to such a place; it must be a rough court, I fear."

"Our Eve going to Paradise Court," said the boy; then the absurdity of the two names struck him, and he burst out laughing.

"But seriously," he went on, "I assure you, mother, Paradise Court is not a place for Evelyn, however suitable she may be in name. What on earth is she going to that wild region for?"

"I want to visit a sick woman who lives there, and who seems to have no friends," Evelyn said brightly. "Surely I am old enough to take care of myself?"

A long whistle was the boy's only answer, as he settled himself to the table covered with books and maps. Then he said,

"Of course, if mother sees no objection, I can't say a word, but I wish she could see the court and its inhabitants."

"I think, dear, we will ask Mrs. Green to go with you tomorrow," Mrs. Moore said quietly. "She will introduce you to your sick woman. I should not like you to go alone, after what Harold says, and you must always go early in the afternoon, before the men return home."

Mrs. Green willingly consented to take Evelyn the next day, and introduce her to the sick woman; and thus it came to pass that she was sitting beside Betsy Martin, singing her a hymn, when little Nell appeared outside the door. There the child remained for some seconds, listening to what she thought was the most beautiful music she had ever heard in her life.

Much too timid to enter and face a stranger, she would have remained crouched up against the door, had not Betsy caught sight of the girl when she opened her eyes and turned to thank her visitor.

"Come in, Nell, come in," she said, as she saw the child still hesitate. "Come in and speak to this kind lady." Then turning to Evelyn, she added, "This is Nellie Jackson, who lives next door; she often comes in to see me."

Very shyly Nell advanced, and Evelyn spoke a few kind words to her; words which the little girl never forgot, for she was not much used to kindness.

But neither of them had any idea what this meeting meant for them both, nor what great results would spring from that small beginning.

CHAPTER 3

HER FIRST PRAYER

Mrs. Moore and Harold were much interested in hearing of the encounter with Nellie Jackson, and Evelyn was delighted to find that her mother had no objection to her calling to see the child when next she visited Betsy Martin.

It was some days, however, before she could find time to do so. When she was at last able to go to Paradise Court, she asked Betsy to tell her more about the girl, whose sad, pathetic face she could not get out of her mind.

Betsy was pleased to secure a friend for her little favourite, so she gladly told her visitor all she knew about her.

Finding her way to the room on the second floor of the house, where the Jacksons lived, Evelyn knocked at the door. It was opened by Nellie, who looked surprised to see a lady standing there, and dropped a curtsey.

"May I come in?" asked Evelyn. "Are you all alone, Nell?"

"Yes, please, ma'am," the child answered, setting a chair for the visitor and wiping it with her frock. "I be mostly alone. Mother's always out at work, and father's with his barter"

"And don't you go to school?"

"Sometimes, please, ma'am, but I ain't strong, and so I often has to stop at home."

"What do you do all day, little one? Can you read?"

"Not a deal, ma'am, only little bits of words. I does nothing all day, except tidy up."

"And who looks after you when your mother's out?"

"Please, ma'am, I looks after myself."

Poor wee mite, she looked so unequal to the task that Evelyn's heart ached for her.

"Do you ever go to Sunday school, Nell?"

"No, ma'am, never."

"Would you like to come next Sunday to my class of little girls?"

"Ever so," said the child, with a bright look on her face. "Will yer ask mother if I may?"

"That I will. Do you know who made you, Nellie?"

"Please, ma'am, God up in heaven; but I

never seed Him, though I often looks up into the sky of nights."

"No one can see God, Nellie; but long ago the Son of God, Jesus Christ, came down from Heaven to teach us to be good. Do you know about the Lord Jesus, my child?"

"Not a deal, ma'am. Betsy talks to Him, but I never does."

"I often speak to Him, Nellie. He loves us to tell Him everything. Jesus loves you and wants you to love Him."

"Do yer think, ma'am, as He knows me among all the folks 'ere in Lunnon?"

"Yes, and He calls you by your name. I think little Nell's name is known among the angels up in Heaven."

"Be it? I'd like them beautiful angels to know 'bout me and love me. Folks say they took my Baby Jess right away up to God. I'd like to see her again."

"So you will, Nell, if you love Jesus, and go to live with Him some day. Baby Jess is with Him now, safe in the arms of Jesus. The dear Saviour loves you so much, that He sent me to tell you all about Him. We will kneel down now and speak to Him together."

So the two knelt down, and Evelyn offered up a few simple petitions for the little untaught one at her side.

Then promising to try and see Mrs. Jackson at the house where she was that day washing, she left Nell, her heart full of an earnest longing to lead this little ignorant lamb to the Good Shepherd.

To Nellie herself it was a day never to be forgotten, especially when her mother returned at night and told her she might go to school the following Sunday afternoon.

Then she would be able to see this kind lady every Sunday, and to listen to her pleasant voice; and she would learn more about God who lived in Heaven. It seemed too good to be true, and before she lay down on her little straw mattress that night she knelt down by the window, and looking up into the sky, where some bright stars were shining, she uttered her first prayer.

"I thank you, kind God, for sending that beautiful lady here, and for letting me go to school. Please take care of Baby Jess what's up with you, and make me a good girl. I want to please you, I do, 'cause you loves me so."

Then this ignorant little one lay down to sleep with a feeling of rest in her heart which she had never known before, and all night long the angels watched tenderly over her, for are they not all ministering spirits, "sent forth to minister to those who shall be heirs of salvation?" And was she not already groping after Him, who said, "Suffer the little children to come unto Me, for of such is the Kingdom of heaven?"

CHAPTER 4

A PRISONER

Little Nell was awake by five the following Sunday, and very difficult she found it to keep quiet till eight o'clock, her mother's usual hour for rising on "the day of rest."

After helping Mrs. Jackson to clean and tidy up the room, and to do some washing (for Sunday was the great day at the wash-tub in Paradise Court), Nellie spent the rest of the morning in making herself tidy, and at two o'clock, with a face that shone as much with soap and water, as with hope and joy, she started off to the Sunday school.

At first the quiet and order of this school, so different from the ragged school she had attended, rather alarmed her; but Miss Moore's kind words and manner reassured her, and she was soon listening attentively to what was passing in the class.

The subject chosen by Evelyn for that afternoon's lesson, chosen no doubt with some reference to little Nell, was the story of the Good Shepherd, and very earnest became the child's face as she heard that the Good Shepherd had laid down His life for the sheep. Then a great wonder filled her eyes, when she found that she was one of the lambs for whom the Shepherd gave His life.

At last the little heart seemed full, and with a great sob, she burst into tears. The other children looked on astonished, while one or two of them smiled. They had heard the story so often, that, alas! it had not the same power and charm for them.

Before Evelyn could speak to Nell and try to calm her, the child made a sudden rush. She darted down the schoolroom, out at the door, and fled away home. Her heart was full, and she longed to be alone; so making her way to a deserted shed in the court, which had often proved a friendly hiding-place, she sobbed for some time without restraint.

To think that anyone had been so good and kind as to die for her. It seemed too good to be true, for hers had been such a loveless childhood. She longed to hear more of this wonderful love; but then the sad thought came, would the lady ever forgive her, and let her come to her class again?

Nell thought she had reached her hiding-place unobserved by anyone, but, alas! Jim Turner had seen her from a corner of the court, where he and two or three other lads were playing marbles. He saw where she went, and just as she was thinking of peeping out and trying to steal into the house, she heard footsteps outside, then a grating sound, and she knew that she was being locked in with a padlock, which sometimes did duty on the old door. With a loud cry she pushed against it with all her might. It was fast, and she realised that she was a prisoner, at the mercy of Jim Turner.

"Let me out, Jim!" she screamed; "let me out!"

"No fear," was his answer, putting his mouth against the door. "You're in now, and there you'll be. I'll teach you to run away from me. Yer can't now. I hope yer will enjoy the night"—and he laughed rudely.

"The night!" Was she to be left there all night; would no one come and let her out? Again she pushed with all her strength, she shouted, and begged to be released, all in vain. She heard the footsteps die away, and knew that no one could hear her. The shed was at the top of the court, and was used by some of the men for their barrows and vegetables, but they were not likely to come that night, for they would not need their things till the morning.

For a long time she continued to call loudly for help, hoping that someone might be passing and hear her; but at length, worn out with her efforts, she sank down on the straw, sobbing bitterly, her heart full of angry thoughts against Jim.

Gradually her passion subsided, she grew calmer, and then she tried to remember what she had that day heard in school. The Shepherd, she had been told, was good and kind and gentle, yet they had put Him to death. He had borne it all patiently, and prayed for those who killed Him.

She couldn't pray for Jim; she hated him; but she tried to think of the Good Shepherd's love, and it comforted her, for she was getting frightened and timid all alone.

It was almost dark now, the short December day was closing in, and the only ray of light in the shed came from a hole in the roof where some of the tiles had fallen off. It was very cold, too, for snow had been falling all the day, and her limbs began to feel numb and stiff. Was there no means of escape through that hole? The sudden thought struck her; at least she would see if this were possible. So groping her way along the wall, she came to a rope hanging from a beam. This she thought would be useful. If she could only mount up by its means, she might climb out on to the roof and slip down outside the shed.

Could she do it? She was stiff with cold and weak with hunger, but at least she would try. Anything was better than staying there all night.

To herself she said, "Perhaps the kind

Shepherd will help me; I'll ask Him." So kneeling down on the straw and putting her hands over her eyes to hide away the darkness, she whispered

"Good Shepherd, thank you for loving me so much as to die for me; please take care of me tonight, and help me to get safe home, and help me to forgive Jim like you forgave them as killed you."

Then rising from her knees, with a lighter heart, she looked about to see the best way to begin her perilous ascent.

She found a piece of wood where she could place her feet. This she managed to do, holding tightly to the rope.

Then, feeling along the wall, she discovered a small ledge higher up, and this with some difficulty she reached. Now she was close to the roof, and could, with a spring, get her body through the hole, which was at a little distance from the wall. Grasping the rope as firmly as her cold hands could, she swung herself to the opening, and tried to catch hold of the side. At that moment, when escape seemed within her reach, the rope slipped from her numbed fingers, and the next moment she was lying a senseless, bleeding form on the floor of the shed.

* * * * *

At five o'clock the next morning, Jim Turner slipped out of bed to unlock the shed and let Nell out before the men came for their barrows. Being Monday, he knew they would not want them early, for they had hardly recovered from the effects of their Saturday and Sunday drinking. As he opened the door, he said roughly,

"Had a good night, little 'un? Perhaps yer won't run away next time. Speak, will yer?" he continued, peering into the darkness, seeing and hearing nothing. But there was no reply, neither a movement nor word of response. At first the boy thought that Nell was hiding to vex him, and he grew angry, and threatened to beat her if she did not come out.

Finding all his threats useless, he struck a match to see where the child was. For a moment even Jim, the bully, stood appalled, for there on the straw lay Nellie in a heap, motionless and apparently lifeless. Her face was very white, while the blood on her head and on the straw, increased the ghastliness of the scene.

Was she dead? That was his first idea. It certainly looked like it. His second thought was, "Well, I ain't to blame, 'twas her own fault," and turning on his heel, he made his way back to bed.

Two hours later the poor child was

found by one of the costers coming for his barrow. He was shocked at the sight, and fetching another man, they conveyed Nell, as tenderly as they could, to her little straw mattress in the back room of the second floor at "No. 4."

Jackson was still asleep in the corner; his wife was not at home, having been up all night with a sick neighbour; hence her not missing the child.

At length, fully aroused and fairly alarmed, Jackson went off to seek his wife and to bring a doctor; but, with all their efforts, it was some time before consciousness returned. The doctor feared concussion of the brain, and ordered perfect quiet for some days. Alas! how was this possible in Paradise Court?

CHAPTER 5

MEMORIES OF THE PAST

Evelyn longed to follow little Nell, when school was over, in order to comfort the tender heart, which she saw that day had awakened for the first time to a Saviour's love; but there was other work awaiting her at home.

The hour after school on Sunday afternoon was always spent by her mother's sofa, and nothing must interfere with that hour of quiet communion. Then came tea, and some sacred music with Harold, before he took her to the evening service.

The next two days were taken up with teaching and home duties, and it was not till Wednesday afternoon that she found herself at liberty to go and visit her little scholar. Before she reached the Jacksons' room, Evelyn heard from the neighbours that Nellie was ill, and when she knocked, the door was opened by Betsy Martin, who had crawled out of bed to come and sit beside the sick child while Mrs. Jackson went out to work.

Nell was awake, and her face lighted up as Evelyn sat down beside her. Hearing from Betsy that she was still to be kept very quiet, she only said a few kind words and left, promising to call again the following day.

Each afternoon that week she managed to find time to spend a few minutes with Nellie, bringing her some little comfort or dainty to tempt her appetite. Each day she found the child better, for the brain attack, dreaded by the doctor, had been mercifully warded off, and by the end of the week Nellie was able to creep out again, looking indeed more frail and delicate than ever, but otherwise seeming none the worse for her recent imprisonment and fall. Of the cause of her accident she had never spoken, nor had Jim confessed his share in it; but he managed to keep out of her way, for at the bottom of his heart he felt somewhat ashamed of his unkind conduct.

Evelyn was pleased to find Nellie anxious to hear more of the Saviour, and very interesting it was to teach such an attentive pupil. One day the child asked her to tell her again the story of the Crucifixion, and about Christ forgiving His murderers. When it was finished, the child asked earnestly, "Must us always forgive them as is unkind to us, ma'am?"

Evelyn assured her that we must forgive, if we hoped to be ourselves forgiven.

Nellie was silent, and for some minutes remained very quiet, and her visitor, fearing she was tired, soon left her. But it was not fatigue which made her so still. Nellie was in deep thought. Then she must quite forgive Jim all his unkindness, and his locking her up in the shed. She knew she wanted the Good Shepherd to forgive her, but she knew also that in her heart she was still angry with Jim.

That night Mrs. Jackson was awakened in the middle of the night by hearing sobs. Fearing that Nellie was worse, she was just going to speak, when she overheard the child talking as she thought to herself. She listened; the sounds came from the window, where, kneeling down, the child was praying.

"Dear, kind Shepherd, I do love you; thank you for dying for me. Please forgive me all my sins, and wash my bad heart whiter than snow; and—please help me to forgive Jim, and make me love him, 'cause I don't, Lord, and I want to, ever so."

Mrs. Jackson could hardly believe her ears. She had never before heard Nell pray; certainly she had never taught her child, for it was years since she had knelt in prayer herself. As she listened, her thoughts went back to the little village in Yorkshire, where she was born, and to her happy cottage home. She saw herself once more a child, sitting at her mother's knee, and hearing from her dear lips the Bible stories she then loved so well. How little in those days did she think that her present joyless, weary existence was possible! Her whole life passed in review before her, and long after little Nell had crept noiselessly back to bed, and had fallen asleep did her mother lie awake, living over again her life's story. She remembered the day, when against her mother's will, and knowing little of his character, she had married Tom Jackson, and come with him to London. She went over all the years since that time—the weary years, the downward steps, as gradually her husband had learnt to spend all his earnings in drink, and she wondered if she had done all she could to win him from his evil ways. How often she had been angry and cross with him; how often her sharp words had driven him further away, and sent him to spend more time and money at the public-house.

As she thought of all this, and remembered her mother's prayers, her mother's holy life, her heart smote her, and burying her head under the clothes, she wept tears of shame and sorrow.

Before she fell asleep, she echoed her child's words: "Please God, make me a better woman; forgive me all the past, for Jesus' sake, and help Tom to give up the drink."

It was many years since Nell's mother had offered up a prayer like this.

CHAPTER 6

FORGIVING AND FORGIVEN

A week passed away, when one day Evelyn found Nellie busy, trying to clean up the room. She was growing stronger now, and was anxious to make the home brighter and more attractive for her father. A comical little figure she looked, in a huge apron of her mother's, and her feet encased in pattens. She was scrubbing the table, and did not see her visitor till she stood beside her.

"You'll make a nice little servant someday," was Evelyn's greeting. "I see you know how to clean a room."

Nell got down from the stool on which she was standing, her face beaming over with pleasure at the kind words. Then she said, shyly, "I'd like to be your little servant when I grow big. I'd try ever so."

"I'm sure you would, Nellie. Well, we'll see about it when you grow older. But I think now you have done enough for today, you look tired. Come and sit down and tell me how you are getting on." Presently she said very gently, "Little Nell, have you yet trusted the Lord Jesus to forgive your sins?"

"Yes, ma'am, I have!" and a bright smile lighted up the little face.

"Tell me about it—how was it?" asked Evelyn.

"It were last night, please, ma'am. I couldn't sleep, and I was thinking of what you said the other day about His forgiving them as was unkind to Him, and I asked Him to help me to do it; and then it all came plain, and I seemed to hear Him say, 'Little Nell, your sins is forgive;' and I says quite low, 'Thank you, kind Shepherd,' for I was sure it was Him; and I've been glad ever since."

"Thank God," was Evelyn's fervent reply. There is joy among the angels today, because the Good Shepherd has found His little Lamb. We will thank Him together for His great love "—and kneeling down, Evelyn offered a short but hearty thanksgiving for this child who had taken God at His word, and trusted Him.

As she was leaving, Nell said, "Please, ma'am, may I ask you something? Betsy says you won't mind."

"What is it, Nellie ? You need not be afraid to ask," Evelyn said kindly.

"Please, ma'am, I wants to make two wool things for the neck; would you show me how? Betsy can't make 'em, and I wants 'em afore Christmas."

"I think we can manage that. I will bring a peggy and some wool tomorrow, and you shall have your first lesson. I suppose you want to give your father a Christmas present, and who is the second one for?"

"Please, ma'am, don't ask, it's a secret," said the child shyly,

"Very well, then I won't ask any questions." Inwardly she hoped it was not intended as a present for herself.

The following day Nell had her first lesson on the peggy frame, and so quickly did she learn, that two days before Christmas the two comforters were completed; and very proud was little Nell, when on Christmas Eve, Evelyn came to finish them off for her. She could hardly believe her eyes when she saw them both laid out on the table ready for wear.

Evelyn had not been idle either, for in

her spare moments she had for some weeks past been making a frock for Nellie, out of one of her old dresses, and the child's joy may be imagined when her kind friend unpacked a basket she had brought with her, and from it took out several parcels. First there was a nice warm frock for Nellie; then followed some tea and sugar, and lastly a plum-pudding.

Nell's eyes were opened wide with delight.

"Be they all for us?" she asked when she had recovered somewhat from her surprise. "What a Christmas we'll have, for mother said maybe she'd bring home a bit of meat." And when she heard that both the frock and pudding had been made by Miss Moore herself, "with her own hands," her gratitude was unbounded.

"Thank yer ever so, ma'am; it were good of yer," she said. "We've never had a

Christmas like this afore."

When her visitor left, Nellie still stood gazing at the things before her as if she were riveted to the spot. Such good fortune for them. A whole half-pound of tea, instead of one ounce; a pound of lump sugar, a warm frock, and most wonderful of all, a plum-pudding! and then those two comforters! It seemed too good to be true. What a rich little girl she felt ! The tea, and sugar, and the pudding she put away in the cupboard; the dress she laid carefully in a drawer, and then she sat and looked at the two comforters, her first piece of work. One was red, the other violet. She stroked them tenderly till the tears came into her eyes. How many prayers had been offered while she made them, for they each had a work to do for God. To her they seemed almost sacred. She determined to give the violet one, as most suitable, to her father; the red one would be more attractive she thought for a boy. Having decided this knotty point, she laid them both with much care underneath her frock, where she thought no one would see them, Then she sat down to wait for her mother, who had promised to come home early, and to bring a "bit of meat for a stew." How surprised her mother would be, and what a Christmas Day they should have!

CHAPTER 7

NELLIE'S SECRET

Christmas morning dawned clear, cold, frosty, and bright. The winter sun, it was true, had not much warmth, but it cheered and gladdened the world with its rays, so that even Paradise Court looked its best that Christmastide.

Nellie woke with a light heart, for she had important business on hand, and two secrets all her own, to be divulged that day. She and her mother had agreed to say nothing about the pudding before dinner, so that it should be a surprise for her father; but she had another surprise for him before that.

Jackson, for a wonder, had returned home sober the night before, and so was quieter than usual that morning.

About nine o'clock he wanted his breakfast; Nellie made him some toast, and waited upon him with such a bright face, that at last her father said,

"What's up, lass ? thee looks well this morning ! "

"It's Christmas Day, dad," she said brightly, "Jesus' birthday;" and she added in a lower voice, "Will you make Him glad today?"

"What do you mean, child? 'Tain't likely I can do that."

"You can; come with me to church this morning. Teacher asked us to come—will yer, dad?"

"I can't, I've no clothes fit, even if I had

a mind, which I haven't."

"Teacher said clothes didn't matter. We could come just as we was, 'cause it's a church a purpose for us poor folk. Won't yer come, father? He do love us so, and it would please Him."

"Not today I tell yer. Give me some more tea!"

Nellie said no more, but when breakfast was over and cleared away, she went to the drawer, and taking from it one of her treasures, she stole quietly behind her father, saying, "Dad, shut your eyes till I tell yer to look; quite shut, don't peep;" and then she put the violet comforter round his neck, and told him to open his eyes.

"What's this?" he said, fingering it. "Where did you get this thing? It's real pretty."

"It's for you, dad. I made it all myself for you. Won't it keep yer warm? You'll wear it, won't you, for Nell's sake?" she added wistfully, remembering the pawnshop where so many things disappeared.

"I will, lass," he said, "it's real nice, and warm too," he added, stroking it tenderly. "You're right down clever to have made it. Who taught yer?"

"Teacher," she said proudly. "Ain't she good? I do love her."

Turning to his wife, who was already at the wash-tub, making use of the home day, he said, "I say, missus, ain't it fine? Do yer see what the lass has made?"

"I see," she said, continuing to rub the dress she was washing. "Now she must make one for herself to keep her warm."

"Oh, mother, I've got a nice warm frock. I'll never feel cold no more."

An hour later, the child, having put on her new frock, and peeped into the drawer to see that the other comforter was safe, was ready to start off for the little Mission Church, where Miss Moore had told her there would be a service especially for the poor that morning. Before starting, she went and stood beside her father's chair. He was smoking a pipe over the fire, and putting her arms round his neck, she said,

"I wish you'd come too, father; it's lonely being by myself."

"No, child, no, not today; perhaps someday when I've better clothes I'll come."

Looking into his face rather sadly, she said,

"I wish yer loved Jesus, dad; He loves you so, and He died for you."

The man laughed as he answered,

"You're turning saint, I declare."

But Nell was gone, her heart sad to think that he had failed in this her first effort to win her father.

Had she failed? Could we have looked into the man's heart, when about twelve o'clock he sauntered out, pipe in mouth, we should have seen that Nell's words, "He loves you and died for you," haunted him, and that there was a tender spot even in that rough heart for his little daughter. He wished he could be a better father, but then, he could not give up the drink. Anyway he determined, for Nell's sake, to have none that day.

Passing through the court on the way to church, Nell caught sight of Jim Turner cleaning his boots on the doorstep of the house where he lived, a little higher up the court. He had his back towards her, and she knew he had not yet seen her; so, quick as thought, she darted upstairs, and opening the drawer where the red comforter lay, she took it up tenderly, and ran down again. On her way, shall I confess it, she kissed her treasure, whispering, "You're to go and make Jim see as I forgives him."

Approaching the boy quietly, she threw it over his head, saying, "Wear that, Jim, it will keep yer warm," and before the lad could turn round, she was off out of the court, and into the street beyond.

Nellie never forgot that bright Christmas service, the first she had ever attended. When the young clergyman told the people that they could all give joy that day to the Saviour by giving Him what He cared for most, their heart's love, little Nell, from the quiet corner where she sat, whispered, "I do, dear, kind Shepherd; I give Thee all my heart," and a great peace and calm stole over her. She hardly heard the rest of the service, but she knew that she had crept to the feet of the Saviour, and laid there her little birthday offering—all she had to give; and few went home from that Mission Church with a gladder heart than Nellie.

As she was wearily mounting the stairs which led to their room, Jim Turner suddenly stood before her. He had been watching for her, and now rather sheepishly thanked her for "the wool thing," adding,

"What made yer give it to me, for I've been a bad 'un to you?"

Very softly but with a bright smile, Nell said,

"I love Jesus, and I asked Him to make me love you. I'm glad yer like it, Jim. Mind yer wear it to keep yer warm."

"Where did yer get it, Nell?"

"I made it."

"You!" said the astonished boy. "You made it, and for me! Well, it were good on yer. Thanks," he added, as half ashamed to have said so much, he ran quickly down the stairs.

And now for the next surprise this glad Christmas Day. Jackson had come in, but he was not in a good humour. He was cross and irritable. The fact was he was beginning to feel he had not been a good husband or father, yet he was not willing to give up the drink, which was the cause of it all.

"What's that on the fire?" he began, "it smells good. Yer seems to find money somewhere, missus."

"That's a secret, dad," said Nellie, as Mrs. Jackson placed a dish with some meat stew on the table. "You'll see what's coming presently."

Jackson said no more, and as his wife was too tired to talk, it was rather a silent meal. At last, after finishing the stew, the plum-pudding, with a bit of holly at the top, was produced, and even Nell was satisfied with her father's look of astonishment. It certainly was a long time since such a dinner had graced the Jacksons' table.

"Where did it come from?" the man asked.

Nell's eyes fairly sparkled as she told him of Miss Moore's visit, and of the various parcels she had brought; and so the meal ended brightly and pleasantly.

After dinner Jackson prepared to go out; with a little coaxing, however, Nellie prevailed upon him to stay at home and read to her, and soon he became really interested in the book Miss Moore had left for him. After reading for an hour, he grew sleepy, and was taking a nap, Nellie still on his knee, when there was a knock at the door, and Evelyn came in to wish them a happy Christmas. At first Jackson was sulky and refused to speak, but soon his visitor's kind words and pleasant manner won him; he became friendly, and before she left, Evelyn had made him promise to come to a

Mission Service, held on Wednesday evening, where she played the harmonium.

When Miss Moore left it was time for tea, and after that, Tom became so sleepy (he was not accustomed to three meals in one day), that he soon proposed going to bed; so that by eight o'clock that Christmas night, the Jackson family were asleep in the back room, second floor, of No. 4, Paradise Court.

Nellie's dreams that night were very bright. She thought her father had become quite good, that they all went to live in a beautiful country village, and that, as the story books say, they lived happily ever after.

But it was not through smooth and flowery paths that God would lead little Nell on her Homeward way, for

"God through paths they have not known

Will lead His own."

CHAPTER 8

THE POT OF SNOWDROPS

It was the last day of January. The cold throughout the month had been intense, and in consequence there had been a good deal of distress in the courts and alleys of London, for work was scarce, and coals were dear.

There was a good deal of poverty in Paradise Court, but as Jackson had been more sober than usual, his family had not suffered so much as some of their neighbours. Once or twice he had been to the Mission Service, and he would sometimes listen to Nellie when she climbed up on his knee to talk to him; but though he loved his child, he did not yet feel that he could give up the drink even to please her, and so occasionally he still returned home the worse for it.

On this morning, the last in January, as Mrs. Jackson was starting for work (she was cleaning an empty house), she said,

"Nell, I want yer to bring me a can of hot tea about four, that empty house will be cold today, and a drink of hot tea will warm me. I've got some bread and cheese with me, so I shan't want no food."

"I'll come," said the child. "I'll bring yer a bit of toast and dripping," and as she spoke she jumped out of bed to see what sort of morning it was.

"It's snowing, mother," she went on; "you'll get very wet."

"'Tain't far, child—don't trouble about me. If the snow is very bad, don't you come this afternoon. I'll manage."

"All right, mother, I'll come if I can," she answered, as her mother left the room.

That day Nell was busy finishing another comforter, which she was making for her mother, after which she was to begin one for herself. She did not feel well; the intense cold since Christmas had tried her, and in spite of her warm frock, and some flannel Evelyn had given her, she suffered much from the inclemency of the weather. She began to think over her last Sunday school lesson, when Miss Moore had spoken of the Lord Jesus coming again to fetch His people. She had told the children that He might come at any time, and urged them to be ready. Then she asked them to remember three things: they were to be washed, to be waiting, and to be working. Washed, and so forgiven; waiting, and so ready; working, and so occupied in His service till He come.

As she worked on, she tried to

remember every word, and softly to herself she whispered,

"Lord Jesus, I want to be quite ready when Thou dost come. Wash my heart, and keep it clean every day, and please make father and Jim love Thee."

Thus she prayed, little thinking that her quiet Christian life and example were doing a work for God in those two hearts, which eternity alone would reveal.

Then she got out her book and began to spell out a page, that she might be ready for Miss Moore when she came again, for the latter was teaching Nell to read. Her progress was slow, but it was sure, for she took great pains to improve.

While thus engaged she heard steps on the stairs, followed by a knock at the door, and on opening it, she found Jim Turner standing outside, a pot of snowdrops in his hand.

"May I come in, Nell?" he said, somewhat shyly. "I've something here maybe you'd like."

"What, them beauties for me! Oh, Jim, how did you get 'em?"

"I bought 'em," he answered rather proudly. "I've been saving up halfpence for a month, and now I've got it. Ain't it a beauty?"

"That it is. Oh, Jim, it's real kind on you, thank yer ever so;" and she looked lovingly at the white blossoms bending gracefully among their green leaves, as she took the pot out of Jim's hand and carried it to the window-sill.

"It'll get all the sun it can there," she added, "and I can watch it every day growing; it will be fine company."

Jim stood watching her as she moved slowly across the room, and then he exclaimed suddenly,

"I say, Nell, be yer ill? Yer look bad."

"No, Jim, I ain't ill, only so tired; I'm always tired now. Why?"

"'Cause I heard Betsy Martin tell mother 'you'd never been the same since that night in the shed, and that she didn't think you was long for this world.' Be you going to die, Nell?"

"I don't know, Jim, but I don't think so, only I feels more tired than I used to; but it's been so cold lately, maybe that's it."

"I've been wanting to tell yer, Nell," the boy said sheepishly, "I'm real sorry I was bad to you that night, I do hope you ain't going to die."

"I shouldn't mind much if I was, 'cause then I should go to Jesus and be with Him for ever."

"Shouldn't you be afeared to die then?" he asked with astonishment.

"No, 'cause I know Jesus loves me, and I'd like to be always with Him."

"Lar, it must be nice to feel so. I'd like to. I'm awful feared to see God. Ain't you feared He'll be angry?"

"No," said little Nell, with an earnest look in her big eyes, "not now, 'cause though I've been real bad, Jesus has forgiven me, and washed away my sins. My heart was black, but Jesus washed me white as snow; " and as she spoke, she pointed to the fast falling flakes which were descending outside. "I like the snow," she went on, "cause it reminds me of a text teacher taught me the other day, 'Wash me, and I shall be whiter than snow.'" Then looking earnestly at her companion, she asked gravely, "Jim, will you pray that every day? I know He'd do it for you."

"I'd do most anything for you, Nell," he said, "but I'm feared I'll forget to do that.

Maybe I'll think on it sometimes; but I must be off now, I've to fetch mother's washing."

As he turned to go, Nellie said,

"Them snowdrops will often mind me of what my heart ought to be, white like them, a drop of snow. Thank you ever so; I do love 'em," and she stroked the flowers fondly.

When Jim was gone she carried the plant next door to show it to Betsy Martin, generally the recipient of all her joys and griefs.

At four o'clock she started off with her mother's tea, in spite of the thick snow which continued to fall. Hard work she found it to get along, and her thin little cloak scarcely kept out the cold and piercing wind which almost took her off her feet. But on she trudged, nothing daunted, for "mother would want her tea." She took a long time to accomplish the short journey, but at last she reached the empty house where her mother was working.

Mrs. Jackson was astonished to see her, and glad as she was to have the warm tea, she was really sorry that the child should have come out that snowy day.

Shivering, wet, and weary, she at length reached home, and sat down before the little fire to dry her wet clothes. She had none to change, and so she must dry them as best she could. Her boots she took off, but her stockings were wet through, and she did not think of the, consequences of keeping them upon her feet.

That night the poor child tossed upon her bed, hot and sleepless, and in the morning she was so feverish that her mother asked Betsy Martin to bring her work and sit beside her, as she herself could not afford to lose the day's charring.

Evidently Nell had taken a chill the day

before, for her limbs ached, and her head was racked with pain. After two or three days in bed, however, she seemed better and was able to sit by the fire, but she looked whiter and more delicate than ever. So Evelyn thought, when, a few days later, she found her way to Paradise Court, and the sound of the dry, hard cough, which seemed to shake the little frame, distressed her greatly. However, the child did not complain, though it was some weeks before she felt well enough to leave the house, and during all that time her snowdrops were a continual source of interest and pleasure to her. She spent many hours alone, but she never felt lonely; she loved to watch her flowers, and to talk to them. It was something of her very own to care for and cherish, something alive, and her pot of snowdrops was a constant companion to the lonely child. How she watched the unfolding of every bud; how sad she was when one or two of the flowers faded and died; it was like parting with a dear friend.

That plant seemed to have a softening influence upon the whole family, for to Mrs. Jackson it recalled the old home and the flowers in her mother's garden; while Jackson took almost as keen an interest in every blossom as Nellie did, because he saw the joy it gave to the child, whose life and words were surely but unconsciously influencing his heart and character. He made up his mind that "Nell should always have a pot of flowers to watch over, if he could in any way manage it."

And so passed away the cold, wintry weather.

CHAPTER 9

LOST

March came in that year like a lion, cold, bleak, and stormy, but about the middle of the month there was a change. There came a week of warm spring weather: the wind was soft and balmy, the sun shone brightly, the birds sang in the parks and squares, and all Nature rejoiced.

On one of these days Mrs. Jackson, before starting for her work, suggested that Nellie should go out in the middle of the day and get a little air. "It will freshen you up, Nell," she said; "you look as if you wanted a breath." And truly she did, for those warm spring days seemed to take from her the little strength she still had.

"I'll try, mother," Nell said, "but my legs ache so, I can't go far."

"Well, go for a bit; it will do you good, and the shops will amuse you."

So about twelve o'clock, the child crept downstairs and out of the house, taking her way very slowly into the street outside the court.

As a rule she enjoyed a little outing; the shop windows were a great delight to her. There was one special shop at the end of the next street, where dolls of every description were to be seen in the window. How many hours in past days she had spent gazing into that shop, looking with delight at the beautiful dolls, and wondering which she would choose if she had lots of money. Would it be the baby doll with flaxen hair, or the little girl with the lovely hat and feathers? She generally decided in favour of the baby doll, because it reminded her of "Baby Jess;" and then she liked to imagine what the joy would be of possessing that doll, and having it always to nurse and play with.

But today she wondered if her legs would carry her as far, she felt so weak; however, she determined to try. She rested several times as she went along, standing before the shops, and pressing her face against the panes of glass to get a closer inspection of the beautiful things within. Before a baker's shop she remained a long time, for she felt faint, and the smell of the new bread seemed to comfort her.

"It's next best to eating it," she said to herself, as at length she dragged her weary feet away from the tempting display of cakes and buns of all descriptions. Her strength seemed to be growing less and less, yet she struggled on for one sight of that baby doll, which reminded her so much of her little sister in Heaven. At last she was close to her favourite shop, there was only the road to cross now. She waited till a moment's lull in the traffic seemed to make it safe, and then she began to thread her way between the vehicles. As she did so, a hansom cab dashed round the corner of the street, and before the driver could pull up, Nell was thrown down and kicked by the horse's hoofs. In a moment a crowd had gathered round, while one man, evidently on his way to work, picked up the child, and tearing off his necktie began tenderly to stanch the wound on her forehead. (He had many little ones at home, and he loved all children for their sakes.) Someone suggested carrying her home, but no one knew where she lived, or to whom she belonged. What was to be done?

"She must be taken to the nearest

hospital," said a voice from the crowd. "Will two men carry her there? It will be better than the shaking of a cab."

Two men at once volunteered, the working-man being one. So they bore the unconscious form of little Nell, and laid her on a bed in the accident ward at the Middlesex Hospital.

*　　*　　*　　*　　*

That evening there was trouble in the back room on the second floor of No. 4, Paradise Court. Nellie was missing; what had become of her? Her parents were distracted. Inquiries were made. She had not been seen or heard of; nothing was known of the missing child.

It was not till the following day that the news reached Evelyn Moore, and her distress at the disappearance of her favourite was great. That evening she told her brother of the Jacksons' trouble. When she had finished, he said,

"I wonder if that could have been the child I saw taken off to a hospital yesterday, as I was coming down Liquorpond Street. I was told she had been run over and was badly hurt, but I did not see the girl myself."

"Oh, Harold, perhaps it was Nellie. Tell me more about it."

But there was not much to tell, for a street accident is no uncommon thing in London, and Harold had not stopped to inquire particulars.

"Is it too far for us to go to the hospital and ascertain if she is there?" asked Evelyn eagerly.

It was a fine evening, and finding that Harold could spare the time, Mrs. Moore made no objection, for she too felt anxious about the missing child.

An hour's brisk walk brought them to Charing Cross, to which hospital Harold thought the girl had been taken. They found that it was true; a girl of about ten had been brought in the day before, but she was so much injured that it was feared she had not many hours to live. She had been unconscious ever since she came in.

Evelyn's heart sank within her as she listened.

"May I see her?" she asked; "it would be a satisfaction to do so."

No objection was made to this, for the authorities were anxious to identify the unknown child. Leaving Harold downstairs, Evelyn followed her guide through several passages and corridors till she came to the ward where the child lay. The nurse took her to a bed in the corner, but as she approached she hardly dared to look at the figure lying there so still and unconscious, and it was with almost a feeling of relief that she saw it was not the little girl she sought. That golden head lying on the pillow did not belong to little Nell. After a moment's silence, Evelyn said,

"That is not the child I'm seeking; poor wee mite, how sad for her to die with none she knows near her!"

"They couldn't do her any good now," said the nurse, shortly but not unkindly. "She's not been conscious since she came in, nor will be, I fancy."

"I wonder if she has a mother," said Evelyn, as she turned away. She must be broken-hearted not to know where the child is."

"Maybe," said the woman, "but we shall do all that can be done for her."

It was with a sense of relief and yet of

disappointment that she and Harold turned their steps homeward. They had so hoped to have some news for the distressed parents. But two days passed away, and still no tidings came.

It was Saturday morning, and Harold, seeing his sister's anxiety about her favourite scholar, promised to spend his half-holiday in calling at some of the other hospitals on the chance of her being in any of them.

On that same Saturday morning, after leaving her pupils, Evelyn went round by Paradise Court to inquire if anything had yet been heard of Nellie. At the door of No. 4 she saw Jim, who looked anxiously into her face with the question,

"Have yer heard anything on her, ma'am?"

"No, Jim, but I hoped you might have tidings of her for me."

Jim's face fell. "I've been round to all the

police-stations, but I can't hear nothing. Do yer think she's dead?" he added in a lower tone.

"Indeed I trust not," said Evelyn, though her anxious heart almost belied her words. "I think we must hear of her soon."

At that moment a policeman entered the court, upon which there was a general flight of the children, who looked upon these guardians of the law as their natural enemies. However, for a wonder, he took no notice of any of them, but marched straight up to No. 4. He was about to enter, when Evelyn stopped him, saying,

"Would you kindly tell me if you have brought any news of Nellie Jackson?"

"Yes, ma'am, I have; I am now on my way to see the parents respecting that young female."

Jim, who was standing by, drew nearer.

Even his innate dread of a "bobby" disappeared in his strong desire to hear of Nell; and he listened intently as Evelyn asked,

"Is she then found? Where is she?"

"She is reported as being located at the Middlesex at the present time, and they fear she is lying dangerous;" and then he went into the house to give the same information to the anxious parents.

Evelyn followed him up the stairs, but neither Jackson nor his wife were indoors; so she hastened home to obtain her mother's leave to go at once to visit the child.

After taking a hasty luncheon, she started off for the Middlesex Hospital, thankful to feel that the child was found, but wondering much as to her present condition.

Arrived at the hospital, she was taken up to the ward where Nellie lay. But could that be little Nell, so white and death-like, her head bandaged, and her eyes closed? It was indeed she, yet how changed even during the last few days. "Was she dying ?" This she asked the nurse in a low voice as they stood together by the bedside.

"Not at present, we hope," was the answer; "but she is badly hurt; the hip is injured, and the head severely cut. I don't think she is asleep, but she hardly takes notice of anything;" and she gently touched the child's arm lying outside the sheet.

The large eyes slowly opened, and as Evelyn bent down close to the child's head and whispered her name, a look of recognition passed over her face, and she murmured the word "Teacher." Then the eyes closed again, as if the effort had been almost more than she was equal to.

"She hasn't taken so much notice before," said the nurse, who was watching her closely. "I am glad to see that look of intelligence."

"She knew me, so I hope the brain is clear," said Evelyn softly.

As she turned round to speak, she was conscious of a pair of earnest grey eyes gazing upon her from the next bed.

"May I stay with Nellie a little while?" she asked. "She might like to find me here if she opens her eyes again."

"You can stay for a bit, if you like," answered the nurse, "but I doubt if she will rouse again just yet;" and she passed on to another patient.

Sitting down between the two beds, Evelyn said a few kind words to the other child whose eyes were still fixed upon her.

The girl's face brightened as she listened, and she timidly answered the questions which Evelyn asked her about herself. Alas! it was a sad story of neglect and sorrow, for Phyllis

Brown was an orphan, with none to care for her.

Her father, a navvy, had died in a lodging-house in Spitalfields when she was a baby; her mother had remained there, doing odd jobs and picking up a precarious living, till two years ago, when she too had died, evidently worn out with her hard life. Since then, Phyllis had remained as the drudge of the lodging-house, allowed to stay on for the hard work she did; cuffs, blows, and curses had been her portion, and every bit of food had been grudged her by the hard woman, she served.

A few days before, she had fallen downstairs and broken her leg, and glad enough to be rid of her, they had sent her to the hospital, caring little whether she lived or died, or what became of her.

Evelyn did not learn all these particulars

at this first interview; they came out by degrees; she heard enough, however, to know that Phyllis had no one belonging to her, and her kind heart was troubled. She spoke to the child of the Friend who cares for little children, but she found that Phyllis had never even heard the name of Jesus Christ.

As she spoke in a low voice, there was a movement in the next bed, and Nellie's eyes opened. In a moment Evelyn was kneeling by her side, speaking tender, soothing words.

A faint smile answered her; then came the whispered words, "I think I'm going to Jesus."

Before Evelyn could reply, the weary eyes closed again; and feeling she had stayed long enough, she said goodbye to Phyllis, promising to come the following day.

"Going to Jesus!" Was Nellie really dying? Evelyn asked herself as she walked quickly home.

No, not yet, little Nell: your work on earth is not quite finished.

" Not now, my child, a little more rough tossing,

And then the sunshine of thy Father's smile."

CHAPTER 10

THE MESSAGE OF THE LILIES

When Evelyn left the hospital, she fully intended to return the next day and see the two sick children.

But that night Mrs. Moore was taken seriously ill, and for three weeks she lay between life and death. Evelyn never left her, except at night, when an old and trusted servant took her place.

It was an anxious time; there were days when the doctor's face looked very grave, and Evelyn almost feared to ask his opinion of her mother. Then came a rally, only for a day or two, however; then again a relapse, and so the anxious, trying days passed on.

At length, after three weeks of alternate hopes and fears, there was a decided change for the better, and the doctor began to speak hopefully of the future. A few days more, and the invalid was able to be moved to the sofa for an hour or two. Then she insisted on her daughter's leaving her in Susan's care, and going out for fresh air and exercise.

"We shall have to nurse you next, my child," she said, seeing Evelyn hesitate. "You look pale and worn. It will please me if you go out this fine day."

"Well, mother dear, I will, if you really wish it," she said, bending to kiss the pale, thin face on the pillow. "I will go and see Nellie. Harold brought a better account of her yesterday, she seems able to talk a little. How pleased she will be to see me!"

"Yes, go and see her, darling, and take some of these lovely lilies of the valley, which your uncle sent me yesterday. The children will like to have them."

Evelyn was soon on her way to the hospital. She enjoyed the walk. The fresh air seemed to put new life into her, and her heart was full of gladness because her mother was better. She could hardly believe that it was a month since she had seen Nellie; what a weary, sad month it had been!

She found the child suffering greatly, for an abscess was forming on the hip joint; but a smile broke over her face as Evelyn approached the bed.

"This is nice," she said. "I've wanted ever so to see you. Is the lady better?"

"Yes, thank you, dear Nellie, my mother is much better, I am thankful to say; has the pain been very bad?"

"Very bad at times, ma'am, but He helps me to bear it; it's wonderful how He does. 'Tain't quite so bad today, and Phyllis and I, we wants you to talk to us; no one has never talked to her about Jesus."

"Poor Phyllis," said Evelyn kindly, turning to the child, whose eyes were fixed admiringly upon the flowers in her hand.

"Would you like some of these lilies?" she asked.

The child's eyes sparkled.

"Are they for my very own?" she said, flushing with pleasure, as she held out her hand to receive them.

"Here are some for you, and some for Nellie," said Evelyn, giving a few of the lilies to each girl.

Phyllis took hers with fingers that trembled with excitement. They were the first flowers she had ever had of her very own, and they seemed to her the most beautiful things in the whole world.

She looked at them lovingly; she stroked them tenderly; and at last she raised them to her lips and reverently kissed them.

Evelyn was much touched by such a reception of her gift. As she went on talking to Nellie, she heard a sob, and turning round she saw Phyllis in tears, while she whispered to her flowers fond, endearing words.

Sitting clown between the two beds, Evelyn spoke to the children of Jesus and His love. She found that during the past three weeks Nell had taught Phyllis much about the Saviour she herself loved.

Nell's look of quiet happiness, and occasional nods of satisfaction, while Evelyn spoke, were most amusing; while Phyllis, though listening attentively, seemed unable to lose sight of her flowers, and at times continued to stroke them tenderly. These last three weeks had been the happiest part of Phyllis' life. Kind treatment, good food, and the friendship of little Nell, had done wonders for the poor neglected child, and she was dreading a return to the old life of misery.

Presently Evelyn asked, "What makes you love these flowers so much, dear child?"

"Please, ma'am," she answered, "I never seed any like 'em afore, and it seems like God saying, 'I loves yer, little Phil!' I suppose thems the sort as grows up in Heaven, for Nell says it's fine up there. I'd like to go and see 'em all a-growing."

Seeing that Nell began to look tired, Evelyn thought it best to take leave; so she rose to go, promising to come and see them again soon.

As she did so, Nell said,

"I wanted to tell yer, ma'am, that Jim's

been to see me with mother, two or three times; and he's beginning to love Jesus, and I think father is too. Will you go and help them as you did me? What should I do now if I hadn't the kind Saviour always with me, loving me and helping me to bear the pain?"

Promising to do as Nellie wished, and to see after her father and Jim, she left the hospital with a feeling of thankfulness and joy, for she saw that Nellie's life and words were bringing a blessing into many sad and sinful hearts.

CHAPTER 11

PHYLLIS FINDS A HOME

Mrs. Moore recovered her strength very slowly, and in the beginning of May the doctor advised her to try the effect of sea-breezes. Yorkshire was her native air, and he suggested Birling Quay as a suitable place, thinking that it would afford just the tonic she needed.

Accordingly it was settled that on the 10th of May, Mrs. Moore and Evelyn should go to Birling for a fortnight, Harold accompanying them for a few days.

Evelyn had been several times to the hospital, and her visits were always hailed with delight by both the children. Nellie was gradually growing weaker; indeed, at times she appeared to be so near the Golden Gates, that it seemed strange they did not open and let her in; then for a time she would rally, but all knew now that slowly but surely, her life was ebbing away, and that little Nell was drawing very near to her Heavenly Home; and as she came nearer, she grew more like Him whom she was so soon to see face to face. Her sufferings were all borne with a patience and courage wonderful in one so young.

Once when Evelyn found her in great pain, she whispered, "I seems to get to love Him more every day; sometimes, when the pain's awful bad, He comes quite close, nearer than the pain, and He do comfort me so."

And Evelyn understood, as she never had before, a sentence she had once read, which at the time had puzzled her.

"I once thought the strongest thing on earth, that which reached deepest into our nature, was pain; but I have lived to learn that His love is stronger, His peace is deeper than all pain."

It was the 2nd of May, a bright spring morning, when leaving her mother comfortably established on the sofa, Evelyn started off to see the two sick children, and to say goodbye to Phyllis, who was to leave the hospital that week. As she walked along, her head was full of plans about the little orphan. What would become of the child? Where could she go next Thursday? What would her future be? She found Phyllis very sad; she dreaded leaving the hospital and saying goodbye to little Nell, for the friendship between the children was very strong.

When Evelyn had sat for some time beside them, Nellie said, "Please, ma'am, I've something very particular to say to you; can you come quite close?" And when she stooped down to listen, the child said, "I've been thinking a lot about Phyllis and that lodging-house; I don't want her to go back again. You see, when I'm gone, mother will be lonesome, for she won't have no little girl, and I would like her to take Phyllis instead of me. Will you ask her? Try and persuade her, please, ma'am. I'd die happy if I knew Phyllis had a home, and you to see to her. Then she will grow up good, and go to school."

Exhausted with the effort she had made, Nellie stopped and gasped for breath, and Evelyn promised to go and see her mother, and tell her of her child's wish. The fact was, this plan had presented itself to her before, but she had wondered if the home influence would be good for the girl. However, she now determined to see the Jacksons at once, and mention the subject to them. At first she found Mrs. Jackson averse to the proposal. She would not believe that Nell was going to die, and if she did, she didn't feel inclined "to take another brat to look after." But, by a little gentle persuasion, and by the promise of a small payment for the first three months, Evelyn at last obtained a temporary home for the child at No. 4, Paradise Court.

Nell's delight when she heard the news was great. "Now I be quite happy," she said with a smile. "Phyllis will be mother's little gal when I'm gone."

And so the orphan Phyllis found a home with the Jacksons when she left the hospital, and Evelyn rejoiced to see how well the plan worked, "for Nell's sake" being the motive power on both sides.

"For Nell's sake" Mrs. Jackson often spoke kindly to the untrained child who tried so hard to please her; while Phyllis found it easy for love of Nellie to do all she could for Nell's mother.

Even Jackson grew gentle in manner to the girl who loved his sick child, and who, sometimes in the evening, would climb on to his knee and tell him stories of his Nellie in the hospital, and of all she had said and done there.

CHAPTER 12

ON THE YORKSHIRE COAST

The middle of May found Mrs. Moore and her children settled at Birling Quay, The invalid bore the journey better than she expected, and Evelyn rejoiced to see that change of air and scene was doing for her mother what the doctor's medicines had failed to effect.

For the first two or three days she did not leave the invalid, and Harold had to go off alone on his boating and walking expeditions.

One evening he came in with a quantity of fish; he was in high spirits, having had good sport, and at tea he gave his mother and sister an account of his afternoon sail, ending up with, "You'd like the sailor I went out with today, he seems rather a remarkable man, and has invented a new lifeboat, which will turn any way and not capsize. He has taken out a patent for it, and is hoping it may be adopted soon. He's an awfully nice chap, full of interesting stories; quite one of your sort, mother," he added, "a really good fellow. I should like you to see him, Eve."

"One day I'll come with you fishing," said Evelyn, "then I can talk to him."

"I'm going to his house about some tackle tomorrow morning," replied the lad. "Come with me, I want you to see him. He has started a Sailors' Bethel here on the Quay, and it is full every Sunday afternoon."

"What is the name of this man?" asked

his mother.

"David Andrews; he seems quite an authority here among the sailors. Will you come, Evie?"

"That I will, if I can leave mother," she answered brightly.

The following morning the brother and sister made their way to Andrews' shop. He was alone making a boat, and as they entered, he rose and greeted them heartily and respectfully. He was a pleasant-looking man of about forty, strongly-built, with a bright, happy face and sunny smile. He told his visitors all about his lifeboat, and showed them a model he had made of it. Evelyn asked him about the Bethel, and what led to its being opened. He told her that after his conversion some years ago, it seemed put into his heart to get a place on the Quay, where sailors could meet for service on Sunday, and in the week.

"Had you much trouble in getting the room?" she asked.

"I could never tell you, miss, all God's goodness about that Bethel. I heard there was a suitable place on the Quay, and I spoke to the harbour-master; he said it belonged to a Mr. Randall, and I must apply to him. Now Mr. Randall, he lives four miles off, and I was that rheumatic, I knew I could not walk as far, so I knelt down and prayed about it. Well, miss, just as I got off my knees, Mr. Randall's big dog Nero passed by. I looked out, and there, sure enough, following the dog, was Mr. Randall himself. I made bold and hobbled after him, and then and there I got a promise of that building.

"But that weren't the end; we had many againt us, and they said it was unsafe, and tried to make us give it up. Then Mr. Randall, he sent his own architect to see it, and he said it would be safe if we spent £ 40 pounds on it. But how was we to raise £ 40? You'd hardly believe how that money corned in, miss; we never seemed to have to wait for funds.'"

"Have you had much opposition since the work was started?"

"A deal, miss. Why at first we had the windows smashed, and all sorts of things done to stop us. Now these very men are among the greatest friends to the place, such good Christian chaps."

"Have you long been a Christian man?" Evelyn asked.

"Some years now, miss, thank God," he answered reverently. "I hadn't been inside a place of worship for years, when one day I went in with a friend. There was an after-meeting at the end of the service, but I was going away, when a voice seemed to say, 'Turn back,' and I stayed. It was during that meeting that I saw myself a sinner, and that my sins had been laid on Jesus my Saviour. But," he added, "you see I had a praying mother, so it was all an answer to her prayers. Bless her!"

Seeing that Harold was getting impatient to be off, Evelyn rose to go, saying she should like to come again to see him if she might, and then she could hear more of the work.

"Come and be welcome, miss," was his answer. "I'll be glad to see you, and to show you the Bethel too."

That afternoon Harold proposed taking his sister for an hour's row. He was a fair oar, and as the sea was calm, and Mrs. Moore made no objection, they started, declining the company of a sailor who volunteered to go with them. Evelyn was anxious to find a flower which she heard grew on the cliffs, a little way off; so they determined to row there, moor the boat, search for the flower, and then row back again, and be home in time for tea.

It was a lovely day; the sea was like glass, and most thoroughly they enjoyed their row to the little cove, where they were to land.

With some difficulty they drew up the boat on shore and made it fast, then they climbed the cliff by a path used chiefly by the sailors; a somewhat perilous ascent it is true, but they were young, and much enjoyed the adventure.

Reaching the top, they gave themselves up to seek for the flower they wanted. Soon Harold grew weary of the search which seemed a fruitless one, "a wild-goose chase" he called it, so throwing himself down on the grass, he told his sister to call him when she was ready to return, and in a few minutes he was fast asleep. Evelyn was not inclined to give up the search so easily; she walked on, and becoming interested in her task, quite forgot the time, and wandered for some distance along the cliff. Suddenly she looked at her watch, and found it was already half-past four, and they had promised to be back at five. Her mother would be anxious, and perhaps think them lost; how careless she had been!

Quickly retracing her steps, she came at length to her still sleeping brother. He was astonished to find how late it was, and together they began as fast as possible to descend the cliff path. It was slippery from the recent rain, and about half-way down, Evelyn made a false step, and fell, rolling down the cliff-side till she reached the beach below. Harold, who was behind, had no power to save her, and his heart seemed to stand still when he saw her lying motionless on the stones below. Was she dead? Had she broken any bones? How should he get her home? These questions passed through his mind as he rushed down the steep path.

Kneeling by her side, he called her by name, but there was no answer.

Boy-like, he was puzzled what to do, but he knew that water was good in cases of faintness; so dipping his handkerchief in the sea, he carefully bathed his sister's forehead, then he rubbed her hands, all the time begging her to speak and say where she was hurt. But there was no reply. What could he do? No one was about, for it was a lonely spot; no house was in sight, not even a coastguard station! Could Evelyn be dead? If so, he felt sure the blow would kill his mother.

Suddenly, in his distress, the words flashed into his mind, "Call upon Me in the day of trouble," and there, on the beach, by the prostrate form of his sister, Harold knelt and prayed, as he never had prayed in his life before. He asked God to restore her, and to show him what to do. Never had he been so much in earnest; never in all his afterlife did he forget the awful suspense, the terrible strain, of that hour. It was the turning point of his life, the moment when he first realised for himself his need of a refuge in time of trouble, and that that Refuge must be Christ, as a living personal Saviour.

Once more he sought to rouse Evelyn, but without success. His heart almost failed him, when, looking up, he discovered a figure in the far distance. He waited, with an inward thanksgiving that help was near.

As the man approached, he saw that it was a sailor, with a shrimping net. Harold hailed him. The man looked grave when he came up, and heard what had happened.

"'Tain't the first bad accident that path has had to answer for," he muttered, as he proceeded to try and lift the girl in his arms. "Undo her collar, sir, and loosen her things a bit," he said.

Harold did his best, and at last succeeded

in taking off her collar and loosening her dress.

Presently there was a faint sigh, then the eyes unclosed and Evelyn whispered, "Where am I?"

"You've had a fall, Eve; but I hope you're not much hurt. Can you get up?" She tried to move but with a groan she fell back.

"This won't do," said the sailor kindly. "I'm afraid she's a bit hurt—we'll manage to lift her into the boat; and between us we'll soon have her home."

Very gently they raised the girl, and laid her at the bottom of the boat, then they pushed off, and each taking an oar, made for Birling.

The breeze seemed to revive Evelyn, and before they landed she had again opened her eyes and asked where she was; but she seemed dazed, and unable to make out what had happened.

Andrews was on the beach when they arrived, and he helped to lift the girl out of the boat.

Leaving the sailors to carry his sister up to the house, Harold went off quickly to prepare his mother, and to fetch a doctor.

Mrs. Moore, though much shocked, was calm and collected, and had the room ready to receive her daughter when she arrived.

For some hours Evelyn lay as if only partially conscious, taking notice of nothing around her. It was a relief when the doctor came. After carefully examining her, he pronounced that no bones were broken, but that she was much bruised and shaken. He added that the brain had received a severe shock, possibly a blow, which had partially stunned her, and that she must be kept perfectly quiet for some days. He would be able better to judge of her state the following day. He begged Mrs. Moore to go to bed, and let the servant take charge for the night.

Finding she could do no good she reluctantly consented, making Susan promise to call her if there was any change.

There was none till the early morning, when Evelyn opened her eyes, and fixing them on the maid, asked, "Susan, was mother frightened? How is she? Tell me."

Being assured that Mrs. Moore was gone to bed, and appeared to be no worse, the girl seemed satisfied; her eyes closed, and soon her soft and regular breathing showed that she had at last fallen asleep.

From that sleep she awoke about ten o'clock the next morning, much refreshed, and with her brain clear. The doctor was pleased, but he forbade any talking, and insisted on her being kept as quiet as possible.

Harold stayed with his mother during

those first few anxious days, and was a great comfort to her; then he was obliged to go back to London. However, he left his sister improving, and so was able to return to school with a thankful heart. Before he left, he gladdened his mother's heart by telling her of the blessing which had come into his life, and that he trusted he had truly yielded himself to Christ, as his Lord and Master.

Her heart was full as she answered, "Thank God, my son; for this I have prayed ever since God gave you to me. May you remain His faithful soldier and servant unto your life's end!"

CHAPTER 13

CAN IT BE?

It was more than a week after Harold's return to London before Evelyn was allowed to leave the house, but one day she suggested accompanying Mrs. Moore when she went for her daily airing in her bath-chair.

"I am almost strong now, mother," she said, "and I do so wish to go with you to thank David Andrews for his kindness to me the day of the accident."

"Very well, darling, if you are equal to

the walk we will do so. I too am anxious to see that good man, and express my gratitude to him."

Accordingly they made their way to Andrews' shop, and Mrs. Moore thanked him cordially for his kindness to her daughter.

"I was glad enough to be of any use," he said warmly; "'twas a nasty fall, and might have been very serious. I'm right glad to see the young lady so nicely better."

And then the conversation turned upon prayer, and Andrews told them what direct answers to prayer he had received during his life. Mrs. Moore asked him to tell them some, and he related that once he had had no food in the house, and no money to buy any. He went out to pray about it, and when he came home he found that a neighbour had killed a pig, and had sent them a joint. He also told them of a great conflict of will he once had. A lady had asked him to make two boats for a missionary sale. He made them, and was calculating how much to charge for them, when he seemed to hear a voice saying, "Give them;" but he argued, "I have my family to provide for, how can I?" Still something seemed to whisper, "Give them." He took them to the lady, and when she asked the price he said he wished to give them. The next morning he received a letter from a naval architect enclosing five pounds, as a mark of his appreciation for the design of the new lifeboat.

"That's how the Master pays," went on Andrews, "if we'll only trust Him, but that's what we're so slow to do. We trust in fair weather but not in foul! Thank God, He's a Refuge in the storm. I've proved Him so many a time. Bless His holy name!"

Evelyn asked him if he had had a Christian home as a boy.

"Ah, miss, it often makes me sad to look back on my boyhood. I had a godly mother, a better woman never lived; but I were a wilful lad, and would go to sea, though mother was set against it. Father, he'd been dead many years, and mother always brought us up respectably to go to school and church. There was only two of us. I had a little sister, such a nice lassie she was, and so pretty. It very nigh broke poor mother's heart when she went off and married a fellow called Tom Jackson, a good-for-nothing chap, all against her wishes. We never heard nothing of Lucy again.

" When I came back from sea, after a bit, I found mother had took to her bed, quite broke down in spirits, and Lucy gone, no one knew where. It was a bad business, for I could not stay at home, as I was due on board ship. When I left her she seemed quite cut up; she grieved so after the lass, and me going away too! I made inquiries, and found Lucy had gone up to London with her husband; but we never heard where, and while I was at sea that voyage, mother died. The neighbours told me when I came home how she did pray for me and Lucy when she were dying. She said as how she believed we would both meet her one day in Heaven. I often wonder if she knows her prayer is answered for one of us. But I would like to find my poor sister, and see what's become of her. Maybe she's dead, for it's many years ago. But I weary you, ladies."

While Andrews was speaking, Evelyn's mind had gone back to a certain day last December, when she had asked Nellie to find her a Bible that she might read to her. After some hunting, a Bible was discovered on a high shelf, covered with dust. As this passed through her mind she also remembered noticing on the fly-leaf the words, "Lucy Andrews, the gift of her Sunday-school teacher." The name had struck her at the moment, because she had had a schoolfellow of the same name, and though she had never thought of it since, it seemed now to flash back on her memory. Could it be? It was unlikely, yet more unlikely things did happen sometimes. So when Andrews stopped, Evelyn said,

"No, indeed, we are much interested in your story; you must long to hear of your sister. In a court in London which I visit, there is a Mrs. Tom Jackson, whose husband has been unsteady. I have been wondering whether she could be your sister."

"Jackson's such a common name, you see, miss; but could you tell me something more about her? Our Lucy was a rare pretty gal!"

Evelyn could hardly call Mrs. Jackson even good-looking, she had such a worn and anxious face; so she was puzzled how to reply, but she said,

"Mrs. Jackson has good features, she may have been nice-looking when she was young; she is grown so thin and careworn now."

"Do you know where her home was, miss, afore she married? Our home was at Filing."

"No, Mr. Andrews, I do not; but while you were speaking I remembered that I had once seen the name 'Lucy Andrews' in a Bible that her little daughter lent me. I will write and ask her where her home was."

While Evelyn spoke, Andrews buried his face in his hands, then he said in a low voice,

"It do seem strangely like it, miss, don't it? Lucy Andrews married to a Tom Jackson! But I mustn't think too much about it till I hear more. It would be a terrible disappointment to find it weren't true. Has she any children, miss?"

"She has one little girl of ten years old—Nellie, a sweet child. She will not live long, I fear. She is now in the hospital, dying from an accident."

"Nellie, that's short for Ellen, and that were my mother's name; she were always called Nellie. It all do seem to point the same way, don't it, ma'am?" he said, turning to Mrs. Moore, who all this time had been a silent but much interested listener.

"It does indeed, Mr. Andrews. I cannot help hoping that Mrs. Jackson may prove to be your long-lost Lucy, My daughter will write and ask about it, this very day, and we will let you know at once. Now I think we must be going, as I do not wish her to be tired."

As they left the shop Andrews said, "Please, miss, when you write ask if she had a brother David as went to sea. Then we'd be quite sure. My heart feels just full—it will seem long to wait for the answer."

CHAPTER 14

FOUND!

It was the morning of the third day after this visit to Andrews, that Evelyn entered her mother's room with an open letter in her hand.

"Mother," she said eagerly, "it is just as we hoped; Mrs. Jackson is David Andrews' long-lost sister. How thankful he will be!"

"That is good news, my child ; tell me what she says."

Evelyn then read the letter, in which

Mrs. Jackson said she had had a brother David, who had gone to sea; but she had not seen him for years, and that her home had been in the village of Filing, in Yorkshire. She ended by sending her love to her brother, and saying how she would like to see him. In a postscript she added, "Nell is no better; Jackson keeps real steady, and sends his respects, as do me and Phyllis."

"It is strange," said her mother, when Evelyn finished, "that our coming here has supplied a link in the chain, and that thus this good man's prayer for his sister is answered. As soon as I am dressed, you must go and tell him the good news."

David Andrews was quite overcome when he read his sister's letter. Tears were running down his cheeks as he returned it, saying, "Thank ye, miss, but I can hardly yet take it in. To think that my Lucy's found. What a many years I've been praying for her. God is faithful." After a moment's pause he went on, "I feel as if I must see her; writing ain't the same thing. You see there was only two of us, and I want to tell her that mother forgave her, and died praying for her. Do you think she could come down here for a bit, miss? Maybe the sea air would do her good."

"I am sure it would, Mr. Andrews; but with her only child so ill, in fact, dying, I fear she could hardly leave London just now. Would it be possible for you to go up to town for a few days to see her?"

Andrews thought he might manage this, and so after a little talk it was decided that he should start the next morning to spend a few days with his sister.

A week later, Mrs. Moore and Evelyn found their way once more to Andrews' shop. They were leaving Birling the following day, and had come to say "good-bye," and to hear of his visit to Paradise Court.

As usual he was busy at work when they came in, and he greeted them warmly. "Please be seated, ladies. I hoped you'd be here today, for I've got a deal to tell you." And then out of a full heart, he poured forth his story. He told them of his arrival in Paradise Court, of his meeting with his sister, and his grief at seeing her in such a home. He told of the yarn they had spun that night, recalling all the days of their childhood and youth; and, he continued, "Lucy is changed to be sure. She certainly has lost all her good looks, but there, she was my little lassie of old for all that. Poor thing, she did fret when she heard how mother took on about her. She took that terribly to heart, and do you know, miss, I feel sure there's something working in her heart. She ain't satisfied with herself; and she let me talk to her a deal." Then he told them of his visit to little Nell in the hospital, and of the happy time he had had with her.

"She be very nigh Home, I fancy," he

went on—"just upon ripe for the Kingdom—and oh, miss," he said, turning to Evelyn, with tears in his eyes, "she says it's all your doing, and what you've taught her. God bless you a hundred-fold for what you've done for my Lucy's bairn."

"She is a dear child, Mr. Andrews, and from the first she seemed to drink in Divine truth in a wonderful way."

Then Andrews told them how pleased he had been with Jackson; that he seemed to be quite changed under Nellie's influence, and how he and Lucy had promised, after their child's death, to come and settle at Birling Quay, if he could find employment for his brother-in-law.

"You see, miss, I think they might do a tidy little trade in the greengrocery line; for he seems a capable sort of chap now he's steady, and then I could look after 'em a bit, and recommend 'em. It would be nice to have Lucy settled nigh me, and Paradise Court do seem a queer place for decent folks to live in. Do you approve of this plan?" he added, turning to Mrs. Moore.

"I think it will be a capital thing," she answered, "to get Jackson away from his old surroundings and companions, and to start him and his wife in a new place, where they may begin life afresh." Then she told him that they had come to bid him farewell, as they were leaving the following day.

Andrews seemed quite overcome, and grasping Evelyn's hand, he said, "God bless you, miss, for all you've done for me and mine. I'll never cease to pray for you and yours while I live"— and with these hearty words ringing in their ears, they left the shop, and the next day said goodbye to Biding-Quay.

CHAPTER 15

SAFE HOME

Evelyn's first visit to the hospital on her return home showed her that little Nell was indeed, as Andrews had said, "very near Home."

"How like a fair, white lily she looks, just ready to be gathered," was her thought, as she stood by the little bed that warm June day, and watched the pale face, with its almost unearthly look of peace and brightness.

The eyes which were closed, slowly

opened, and looking up she saw Evelyn standing beside her.

A smile lit up her face as she said, "How nice, you've come back. I've wanted you so bad."

"I only returned yesterday, and I am grieved to find you so weak and suffering."

"I gets weaker," answered the child; "I don't think now it will be long afore I see the kind Shepherd, and Baby Jess, and them beautiful angels."

"He shall gather the lambs in His arms, and carry them in his bosom," said Evelyn gently. "Oh, how those arms will rest you, when Jesus comes, Nellie."

"It will be nice to be with Him always. I like to lie here and think of that beautiful Home you've told me about. I shall tell Him when I get there it was you as taught me to love Him," and she looked lovingly at her teacher.

Evelyn's eyes were full as she answered, "God bless you, little Nell. I trust we shall meet again in that beautiful Home one day, and serve Jesus together."

After a moment's pause Nellie said, "Phyllis do seem getting on nicely—Dad's quite took to her. Please, ma'am, talk to her as you did to me. Tell her to meet me up there."

And Evelyn promised to be a friend to the little orphan, and to care for her, for Nell's sake.

Then again Nellie spoke, "There's Jim too, will you sometimes talk to him? He's really trying to serve God." She was too tired to say more, the weary eves closed, and Evelyn soon left her.

As she was anxious to see the Jacksons, the following day she found her way to Paradise Court. She was pleased to find Phyllis looking well and happy, and evidently giving satisfaction.

Mrs. Jackson, too, was full of thankfulness for the improvement in her husband. "He goes out regular with his barter, miss," she said, more cheerfully than Evelyn had ever heard her speak, "We do have something now of a Saturday night. If only my Nell were getting better I'd be a deal happier."

"She will never be better in this world," said Evelyn gently; "but she is ready, and knows she is going to the Home above."

"Nell's ready, that's certain. I only wish I was as ready to go." Then, as if wishing to change the subject, the woman continued, "It were nice seeing David again—it sent me back to when I were a bit of a lass like my Nell. He were that kind, and he wants me and Jackson to go and live nigh him at Birling."

"It seems a good plan," said Evelyn warmly. "You will be lonely when Nell's gone, and your brother will be a comfort to you. Besides, to start in a fresh place will be a good thing for your husband; it will take him away from his old companions."

As Evelyn left the court Jim appeared from round a corner, where he had evidently been watching for her.

Holding out a leaf on which were carefully laid six ripe early strawberries, he said rather shyly, "Please, mum, will yer take 'em to little Nell—she might like 'em? Tell her I bought 'em. They say she's worse. Oh! I would like to see her again."

"I shall be seeing her tomorrow, can I give her a message for you?" said Evelyn kindly.

"Tell her," he said, and there was a choke in his voice, "I mean to meet her in Heaven—and —and it was all her doings," and he half turned away.

"Indeed I will tell her this, Jim—it will make her very glad—she will soon now be in that beautiful Home with Jesus, and we must seek, by God's grace, to serve Him and so to meet her there."

She did not think it wise to say more just then, for Jim's heart seemed full; but she determined to seek him out later, and meanwhile to see what could be done to take the lad away from his present evil surroundings.

Each time Evelyn saw little Nell she seemed weaker and less able to talk, till one day, early in July, when she reached the hospital, the nurse told her that the child was sinking fast.

Despatching a note to her mother to say she might not be home till late, she determined to remain with the child till the Home-call came.

She found Nell conscious, but almost

too ill to speak; yet she welcomed her kind friend with a smile, and pointed upwards.

Kneeling down by the bed, and taking one of the little wasted hands in hers, Evelyn said, "You will soon be Home now, darling. Jesus is coming to fetch His little lamb to be with Him for ever. No more pain and sickness then."

Nell nodded, and Evelyn caught the words—"With Jesus—Nell's so glad."

"Little Nell will soon fall asleep, and she will wake up in Jesus' arms," said Evelyn softly. Then, seeing the eyes close, she sat down quietly by the bedside and watched her.

For some time Nell seemed to doze. Presently Jackson, his wife, and Phyllis came in, and Evelyn moved away that they might be alone with the child. Phyllis had brought a lovely "Boule de neige" rose in her hand, which she gently laid on the sheet by Nell's hand. She had got up very early that morning, had walked to Covent Garden, and had bought the best rose she could find for a penny. She would have it white, because she fancied the roses of Paradise would be that colour. It was her only penny; she had earned it by minding a baby for a neighbour, and her delight was great in bringing her little offering of love to her friend.

After a few minutes Nell opened her eyes, and seeing her parents by her side, she tried to take her father's hand, saying in a faint voice, "Going home! Jesus is coming for little Nell. Come, Dad—Mammy come." Then, catching sight of Phyllis, she added, "Phyllis come too."

Jackson rubbed his sleeve across his eyes, which were full of tears, as he murmured, "Don't ye, little one, I can't abear it; but, God helping me, I'll come to you up there one day, that I will!"

Nell's look of joy was good to see as she whispered, "That is nice."

Poor Mrs. Jackson was sobbing and kissing the little hand lying outside the counterpane.

"Oh, Nell," she said, "it's hard to part; but you'll be a deal better done for there. You've always been a good girl, you have."

A smile passed over the little face as she murmured, "No, washed, made clean; 'Safe in the arms of Jesus.'" Then again she seemed to doze. Half an hour later, the nurse called Evelyn to come quickly, for the child was passing away.

Kneeling beside the parents, they together watched while the gentle spirit took its flight to the Home beyond.

There was no sound save the sobbing of Mrs. Jackson and Phyllis. Suddenly, when they almost thought she had reached the further shore, a bright smile for a moment illumined her face and she looked up with the words, "Jesus, I come, I come." The next moment she had passed into His presence for ever.

Those who were watching her gazed with awe upon the radiant smile, which remained upon her features, and which seemed to tell them of the joy into which she had entered.

"With Christ which is far better," whispered Evelyn, as she stooped to imprint a kiss upon the white forehead. While she did so, she heard Phyllis say, through her sobs, "She never saw my rose; oh, Nell, it was all I had to give you."

Very softly came Evelyn's answer, "My child, little Nell does not need it now; she is in Paradise with Jesus; but up there she knows how you loved her—and the rose shall be laid upon her, a token of your love."

Then, with a few words of sympathy to

the parents, she left the hospital and hastened home.

Two days later, all that was mortal of little Nell was laid to rest, "in sure and certain hope of a glorious resurrection." Among those who followed her to her last resting-place, there were no more faithful mourners than the two children —Phyllis Brown and Jim Turner—who both owed so much to her loving words and bright example.

It did not need much persuasion to get Jackson and his wife to leave Bloomsbury, and go and settle at Birling Quay. Andrews' offer had come at the right time, for they both deeply felt the death of their child, and they were not sorry to leave the old neighbourhood, and start afresh amidst new friends and better surroundings.

When Evelyn went to say goodbye to

them, she found Phyllis much excited at the prospect of going to live at the seaside, for she had never been out of London before. After a little talk about Nell, Mrs. Jackson sent the child away to go and look after Betsy Martin, who was truly mourning the loss of her little favourite. Then she said,

"I wanted to tell you, ma'am, of the wonderful change in my Tom—he seems altogether a new man since that blessed angel was taken. He minded her a lot, and now he says he's set on meeting her again, and means to live as she wished him. And he asked me to tell you, ma'am, as he won't take no more money from you for Phyllis. We feel she's sort of left to us by our Nell, and we'd like her to be as our own in future. Thank you all the same for all you've done so far. For Nell's sake, we'll do the best we can for her; for me and Jackson have got quite fond of the little lass, with none of her own to do for her. Indeed Tom, he's quite took up with the child, he is."

And thus it came to pass that Phyllis found a home at Birling Quay with the Jacksons, to whom she has become a true and loving daughter. Nell's death completed the work that her life and words had begun, and Phyllis is now an earnest Christian girl, a comfort and joy to her adopted parents, who have cause to bless the day when they received the homeless, friendless orphan under their roof.

Evelyn did not forget her promise to go and see Jim Turner again. She found that he had a great desire to go to sea, and after a time she succeeded in getting him taken on board the Britannia training-ship. When last she heard of him he was doing well, and he gives promise of one day being a good and useful man; but he always says that, under God, he owes everything for this world and the next, to the life and words of "Little Nell," and that his first desire to do right dates from the day when she gave him the red comforter, for it made him believe in the reality of a religion which taught Nell to forgive.

And here we must take leave of the Jackson family. We wish them all success and happiness in their new home, and trust that their whole, future may be influenced by the memory of the short but blessed life of

"LITTLE NELL.".

THE END

ABOUT THE AUTHOR

Dorothy Strange was born in a small village on the edge of the Yorkshire Dales. Growing up in a large family in a close community she quickly learned the true values of life, values which she has carried with her and shared out to others throughout her life.

Printed in Great Britain
by Amazon